Felicity

Book 1 in Felicity

To Georgie, for always believing in me and

supporting everything I do

ISBN: 9798479833274

Other books by Faith

Children's:

The Witch's Kitten (Misty #1)

The Broomstick Trials (Misty #2)

YA:

Felicity (Felicity #1)

Adelaide (Felicity #2)

~ **Contents** ~

~ Chapter One ~

Felicity Thorpe, young, plain, studied, and rarely eager to comply with expectations, was of adequate wealth and house, with a kindly family, consisting of three other sisters, and a blessed marriage between the Mr Aloysius Thorpe himself and his affectionate wife, Margaret. In all her eighteen years of experience, never had she suffered from the absence of necessity nor over-exposure to frivolities; such was considered excessive for a girl of her class and age, particularly the annual ball held in a neighbouring town, hosted by once close friends of the Thorpe's known by the vicinity of Bath as the Thompsons, or, to Miss Felicity Thorpe, as a place her presence may never be accepted by her mother. The belief that men bound by matrimony were no longer of importance in terms of their young daughters was almost common in the household; finding a husband was their first and only condition that would satisfy the maternal wants of Mrs Thorpe; Mr Thorpe however held a particular sweet spot for his second eldest, Felicity, who shared in his enjoyment for the skill of writing, and would often find himself persuading his wife to consider the opinions of their daughter.

Opposed to this idea of living, of course, was their Aunt Augusta, a stately lady who had a habit of outliving life, and much to the dislike of Miss Felicity Thorpe, visited far too often to be considered as a satisfactory companion. Mrs Thorpe, although unafraid to admit her admiration for the charitable yet strong-willed Lady Augusta in her presence, would more often than not indicate the irritating faults of the woman in the absence of the woman herself, yet return to a state of adoration when one in company dared to agree. All four sisters and husband knew too well how hypocritical Mrs Margaret Thorpe could be, and consequently spent little time trying to convince her otherwise. Felicity managed to find enjoyment in conversing with her mother on the subject of her grandmother, for what used to cause such turmoil became indifference, despite the mutual dissatisfaction which was apparent between the two women, both with different ideals and outlooks on life.

Of course, much like her behaviour toward her mother, Felicity treated her Aunt only as a temporary trifle, in the hope that one day she would meet the same end as her husband, and consequently free the family of her opinionated demeanour. Each visit by the great lady was relatively similar to the last, and would consist of a long list of flaws in each of the daughters.

In Kitty much was to be discussed, for "she speaks far too much for a young lady of her age, excites herself at the merest mention of something new to do, never has her hair like a young lady should and she completes her chores to a poor standard." Kitty, much like Felicity, did not care much for the Aunt Augusta either, and took pleasure in irritating her Great Aunt, though it was carried out in a childish fashion.

Miss Phyllis Thorpe was "the dearest little child my eyes ever laid eyes on! But I do wish her hair was lighter and her complexion more full. The girl spends far too much time inside, doing all the chores over again her sister has decided to leave incomplete!"

Then, of course, was the eldest, Adelaide, whom, much to the jealousy of the other sisters, somehow had the approval of their Aunt, so much so that she had been left something in the old woman's will. No one quite knew what, but it was the circumstance itself that surprised the family, including Mr Aloysius Thorpe who, along with his daughters, and most particularly his wife, had constantly done everything wrong that was possible for him to do so. Most likely Aunt Augusta's change of heart towards the eldest of the four was due to her marriage to Mr Nicholas Ramsey, a relatively wealthy business man, and the birth of her daughter, Katarina. The only remark that seemed to be of disapproval in reference to Adelaide was her lack of a male heir but her time was not yet up, and she had found herself what should be both a benefiting and joyous marriage for the two of them.

Much less hope was supplied in response to Miss Felicity Thorpe by her Aunt. She was much like her father in the sense that she was ever disappointing, yet she felt no guilt at the expense of these feelings, and would continue to live almost carelessly, as well as hoping to achieve her dream of publishing her own novel. Her Father had only the one published, and the family had seen no apparent benefits to the family income, but the enjoyment for the subject deemed vital to the two kindred spirits, and both vowed it could never be changed by the harsh words of Lady Augusta.

Neighboured to Thorpe Hall, in which the family had lived so happily in for nearing twenty-three full years, was the Edmunds'; they themselves had three daughters: Christiana, Henrietta, and sweet little Arabella, but they also had the son that Adelaide felt she could only wish for: Nathaniel Edmunds. Intelligent would be a humiliating understatement, yet his finances were not considered substantial enough to acquire the approval of the Aunt in his possible engagement to Felicity. Although nothing on the matter had been said, the disapproval had been implied numerous times by multiple members of the family, most particularly by Mrs Thorpe, who believed that a beautiful young lady such as Felicity had the opportunity to raise the social status of the entire family, much like Adelaide had done so with Mr Ramsey to a small degree.

"Do you ever wonder, Mr Edmunds, that life is what we say it to be, and all these problems surrounding us are merely constructs of our own minds? I wonder much upon the subject, yet I feel I shall never have the answer I feel I need to satisfy my curiosity." Felicity avoided the eye contact in which she usually revelled in from the Mr Nathaniel Edmunds himself; he was leaning against the wooden fence, his hands wrapped in his pockets, gazing down at his companion who held a pen and pieces of paper covered in the ideas she had been composing for a new story. His look was filled with awe, which, although avoiding it, Felicity appreciated and reacted with a warm yet embarrassing smile that she could not remove from the moment. "I know you spend far too much time thinking, Nathaniel, and therefore I can be assured you have something to say also."

"Yes, I do."

"Well, perhaps you should share before I continue, as we both know how liable I am to talk right through the day without so much as stopping to think."

"Yet somehow each word from your lips is of somewhat importance to my little mind."

"You flatter me, Mr Edmunds. Yet, you have still not answered my question. I believe you are delaying the time before you are forced to answer so that you may form an answer worthy of confusing the wits of me."

"The wits of you? Oh! Felicity, I would not dare, for we are all aware how significantly, if hauntingly, your intelligence looms over the rest of us. I would rather hear from you more on the subject, if you would."

"I will not. It is your turn to speak, Mr Edmunds." She placed her writing equipment into an adequately-sized satchel bag, and rose so that she could lean against the fence with her friend.

"Then we shall remain in silence."

"Oh! Mr Edmunds, you are more stubborn than I! How you tease me!" On turning around to walk away from the scene, her hand was gripped by the fingers of Nathaniel, and she felt compelled to turn back towards him. How she wished her Aunt and Mother would approve! Friendship would forever be their limit.

"I, the stubborn one? Felicity, dear, you do make some strange accusations! Perhaps I should set your mind right?"

"And how do you propose to do that? Enlighten me."

"Of course." He set off at a run, releasing the hold on his friend within seconds, as she had barely moved either due to her surprise (and consequently she had been unable to physically move) or that she was terrible at running and had not the time to set off quite as quickly. Either way, once Nathaniel had realised this and had stopped to allow Felicity to catch up, the two tumbled down to the floor as Felicity was met with tickles; a very indecent act as Aunt Augusta would say, but, alas! Aunt Augusta was nowhere to be seen and one would struggle to interfere with such display of young love as was in these two bodies, even had the bystander been the strongest man in Bath.

"Mr Edmunds! Oh!" Felicity found herself trapped beneath his body, and immediately felt uncomfortable with the situation after realising all too quickly how it must have seemed to anyone who had the unfortunate pleasure of passing by.

"Miss Felicity!" A voice called out from behind the trees somewhere and the two held still, their breathing being the only noise other than the apparent footsteps from the owner of that disruptive and untimely voice! "Oh! I do apologise, Miss. I did not know you had company." Felicity noticed one of the maids, one of the few who they did not let go after their financial troubles began, stood in an anxious manner. Nathaniel moved almost immediately after the arrival, but the look in his eyes seemed most demoralising and could easily be seen if a person should even glance upon for a mere second; luckily, neither the young Felicity nor the maid had paid any such attention to him, as he was often regarded as no visitor should ever be, much to his anger.

"Am I needed?" Felicity made an unsuccessful attempt to comb her hair back into place and brushed down her dress. All she felt beside her was the still of Nathaniel, clearly agitated yet silent at the disruption. Perhaps her mother had discovered that he was visiting? Or perhaps Aunt Augusta had decided to make an unwanted visit. Either way, her heart began to beat, each pulse fuelling the fear inside of her stomach.

"Yes, Miss. There is a Mr William Giles here to see you." William Giles? The name ran through her mind like the snow falls in her favourite season, but no William Giles was to be found, for she had but few friends and even fewer acquaintances. "They are waiting for your presence in the parlour, Miss."

"May Nathaniel attend also?" Although she feared for the reaction of her mother, or even more so, the possible appearance of her Great Aunt, she already had a reluctant idea of who this man may be, or rather, his purpose for being here. If Nathaniel were also present, then surely no immediate action could be taken, or the process could be delayed even? Though her mother may be rash and self-indulgent, Felicity believed that she would not be rude to the extent that she would ask him to leave, as of course, that would go against her array of hypocritical views in relation to society and its unwritten rules.

"I cannot say, Miss," was her reply.

"Nathaniel, I hope you will stay with me and bear the burden that I believe to be in store for myself. I am incapable of doing anything correct these days; I like to believe that it has been so since my birth so that I can deny myself a large portion of the blame." Our protagonist followed the same trail taken by the servant, hearing the footsteps of an eager and trustworthy friend behind her own.

"I wouldn't dare leave you if you did not wish it, unless of course a certain Lady Augusta was present, then I would have left the town by now, taking a carriage of course as that is one of the many symbolisms of wealth that one can display if they so wish to. You can tell your Aunt that some of us simply prefer the fresh air and nature in front of our eyes, rather than through a foggy carriage window."

"I don't suppose that to be one of your better ideas, Nathaniel. Already I can picture the look on her countenance and – no, I'd rather not. There is still so much to live for!" The two laughed heartily together, the image of the Aunt incapable of being subdued in their minds, and the reluctantly-known truth that her next visit would most likely be shortly.

"I do not understand your strength, Felicity."

"In what way do you mean? I fear I have none."

"You are certain that you will be walking into some negative atmosphere shortly, yet you still find something to amuse yourself with." His declaration had been formed with a long-growing curiosity, one which was hoped there would be some answer or response to so that he may replicate his thoughts of disbelief at her mental strength to the best of his abilities; far too often had his view been subsided. Perhaps it was due to his class in society, but more so was the power which belonged to his three sisters, who could make the boy do anything they please at a moment's notice.

"I may appear that way, yet I do not feel so empowering. I would like one day to write of a character much like myself but one who has a much stronger mentality, and ever so much more beauty and grace."

"I thought grace was not a want of yours? I thought you were determined to rewrite every rule about what women are expected to be?" Felicity's attention towards him rose as she realised that he did listen when she spoke, rather than simply watching her, acting as though he was. "But I do not myself see the use in such a thing, Felicity. There are rules for a reason." Was he really saying this to her? Were these the thoughts he had kept hidden? It certainly explained his silence.

"But," Felicity faltered. "Nathaniel – it is my dream." Had he not supported her this entire time in her ambition to be one of the first female authors of her time, one who would not have to take a male identity in order to be published, but would be published because she had the talent and the passion?

"Is just that – a dream. Don't you see, Felicity? You will never become an author. That is just not what women do." The anger which she usually contained to such a high standard began to bubble inside of her, and she wished so much that she could raise her voice just a little, but that, of course, was not very ladylike of her, and suppose her Aunt was present in the house?

"I'll prove you wrong, Nathaniel Edmunds, just you see. My name will be printed on hundreds of books before you have even committed your life to something." She set off at a quick walk so as to get ahead of him, hoping he would follow her still. As she expected, he did just that.

Moments later, upon entering the house and reluctantly entering the parlour, Felicity found a sight most expected yet strange at the same time, consisting of her mother and father perched upon a seat, and one who she could only assume to be this mysterious William Giles. His head turned towards the doorway on her entrance, but only for a mere second, and his eyes were the only feature visible due to him taking a sip from one of the china cups only used for special occasions – this was mostly on any visit from their Aunt. Despite the generous nature of the family, visits were often rare.

"Felicity, please, take a seat. Ah, Nathaniel. I had no knowledge of your presence on our land. Perhaps you had better take leave for a while, and return some time other; we have important matters to attend to concerning young Felicity here. Doesn't she have a remarkable look, Mr Giles?" Her mother had already forgotten the presence of their other, less important, visitor, but who could blame her, for she knew the exact reasoning behind this William Giles' presence in the family home? "Felicity, what's that on your skirt? Oh, for heaven's sake child, could you look reasonable for once in your life?"

"There is nothing truly remarkable about her appearance, Mrs Thorpe." How could this stranger be so judgemental, as though he had known her as long as the remaining peoples in the room? Had he not the decency to practise common politeness? Felicity turned around for some support from her friend, but, at some quiet moment he had stole away already, leaving her utterly helpless against whatever monstrosity of a plan had been concurred.

25

"Don't you find her complexion rather beautiful, dear Sir? Does she not look as though she were blessed by some form of Angel? Our Father blessed her well, wouldn't you agree?" He turned to look towards her again, but only with scorn and hatred in his eyes. Felicity felt the skin of her face change to some shade of red expeditiously, realising all too late that her dress was not the only part of her appearance that failed to comply with the expectations. – most obvious was the state her hair had become, or the mud on the side of her face. Then a previous thought dominated her mind once more: why was he here? And why did her appearance matter more than usual?

"It is perhaps agreeable at most, Mrs Thorpe." Agreeable had never once before been used to describe such a character as Felicity's, and although it was perhaps a kindly thing to say considering the stains, she had taken it as such an insult to her character that her face turned sour and filled with shock. "I fear my possible wife disagrees." Oh! So, that was the cause of his visiting! Alas! That could only mean one thing that dear Felicity, despite her experienced levels of intelligence, took a moment more than expected to realise, for she had been so distracted by the whole ordeal she had not time to worry about all at once. "Felicity, I have been told little truth about your character in the recent minutes, and I believe you yourself would provide me with a much more sufficient description – an honest one if you may."

"I had best not, Sir."

"And, why is that? Do tell me." There was something more to the man than mystery – something more mysterious than mystery itself, that is. His eyes told a story but what story that was, Felicity had not the knowledge to decipher as of yet.

"Well, if you expect to me be honest, I fear you may not like the answer."

"We all have our faults. Continue." Feeling as though she had no other option, she did so, and, in doing, sparked a curiosity from the dark stranger that had been deemed an impossible occurrence only moments before.

"Well, I – it is safe to say that I have an undeniable interest for the writings of female authors, and would be honoured to one day be worthy of having a place with them in the world." He gave no answer and no explicit response to this unusual declaration, yet Felicity felt that the look in his eyes was urging her to continue further. "Much enjoyment comes additionally from the piano, except I am far from acceptable at the skill and I beg of you do not ask for a demonstration, for I would simply refuse. But all the same, I can admit to enjoying my time on it. What I love most in the world though, is the world itself. Its beauty entraps me as I embrace the orange colours of autumn taking over what was only recently a luscious shade of green. And the wind howls not as though it were a savage beast, but as though it were singing like the birds, as though it will lead us home."

"That was perhaps too much all at once, Felicity," was the expected although almost forgotten about response from Mrs Thorpe; her mind was all in a flurry about creating the most perfect image of her daughter so that she could follow in the footsteps of her sister, and fulfil her duty as a wife, for that was all she was intended for in this world; not writing nor enjoyment.

"I thought it to be rather interesting, Mrs Thorpe. She certainly has an imagination." Although these were the words coming from his mouth, his face did not seem to appear equal with his opinion, and Felicity, despite longing to look to his face once more, stared down at her feet, nervous and ashamed for talking so.

"Imagination can be altered, Mr Giles, perhaps even removed completely," her Mother's attempts were beginning to seem desperate, and she received only narrowed eyes and furrowed eyebrows from their visitor. "She is usually such a perfect young lady, I can assure you, Mr Giles. I am afraid she has been caught off guard today and is in shock. Please forgive her and do not take it into account. She would be a merit to your household."

"I would not go as far to use the word 'merit', Mrs Thorpe, as she is very far from it. Perhaps 'interesting' would be more appropriate."

"Yes, yes, of course! There will never be a dull moment with Felicity at home! Oh! Does this mean you will accept?"

"Mother!" Felicity, although knowing how silent she was required to be at a moment like this, felt all too strongly to abide without some opposition and the knowledge of trying.

"Felicity, hold your tongue." Her father, who usually would side with his daughter, had decided that this was the best option also, and Felicity knew she would be disappointed in herself to a large extent if she were to disobey his wishes.

"I am not yet ready for marriage. There is so much I have yet to do and to see." *And someone else in mind*, she added to herself.

"I propose the union between Felicity Thorpe and myself, Mr and Mrs Thorpe. I also propose the date of May 15th, as my family will be in town at that point and I wish to have a quick procedure so that I can continue with my business with little interruption." Felicity, more so in shock than ever before, stood motionless, her jaw hanging very unladylike, yet with no care for her appearance as usual, and instead, the priority fell on the words fighting to be heard in her mind pushing into her throat.

"Oh! Mr Giles, this is wonderful news! Oh! Felicity is to be married! May I call you William now that I am to be your Mother-in-law?" The woman could barely remain in her seat with the excitement she held for the circumstance, much less had been expected from the outcome with more much more opposition from her insolent child.

"No, you may call me Mr Giles. I must be leaving, I, as usual, have important business waiting in the neighbouring town. I will be in contact with you, Mr Thorpe, as soon as I see fit." He took leave from his chair, and on walking out of the room, he stopped to the side of his future wife. "I hope you will remain this interesting, although perhaps in a cleaner state would be more appreciated." Still motionless by his side, she attempted a small smile, but dared not embarrass herself further by looking into his eyes. There must be something she could do?

After watching him ride from the land in his carriage:

"Oh! Felicity! You almost disgraced us!" was her mother's outburst.

"Are you referring to the fact that my dress is in an unacceptable state, I had a guest over whom you dislike because of his financial status, or the mere fact that I told the truth? I am not the type to marry, Mother, except for love. Do you wish to break my heart, and then watch it fall apart piece by piece? Do you take enjoyment in my suffering, as though I were not human or your daughter, but simply a pawn used for your own benefit? Of course I do not want to discredit our family, but I also do not want to disown myself and my beliefs. My heart already belongs to another; I do not care for this strange man who seems to only care for his own thoughts! He is as selfish as you!" With this, she whisked herself from the room, and left the couple to discuss their plans for their ungrateful daughter, and hope for the future that something decent and beneficial would arise from the situation. Felicity Thorpe, however, was past this hope, and turned to God, asking for some escape, anything to stop this union from causing the destruction of her happiness.

~ Chapter Two ~

Much was in Felicity's mind regarding the events the day had reluctantly brought for her, and despite multiple hours passing since the immediate shock, she somehow still felt as though she had only recently heard the news. Perhaps it was her Mother's constant mention of what would now need to be done in preparation, or the despairing look on her Father's face which demonstrated his disappointment in himself for allowing the circumstance to occur against his daughter's wishes that caused this continuing anxiety. Felicity believed it to be the unknown which was at fault of prolonging the pain, for she did not know the thoughts of Nathaniel on the subject, or whether he would visit again soon – or perhaps ever – and she did not know much about this William Giles or married life other than what she had been exposed to from her parents and sister. She did not believe herself to be capable of envisioning the perfect wife, let alone to be one, and she always had in her mind that if she ever did wed, it would be to someone she felt comfortable with.

In order to voice these feelings to someone in which there was a possibility of an act of listening, she whispered to her sister:

"Kitty, are you awake?" Her gaze held the ceiling, the peeling paint in her concentration but she listened for movement of some sort and a reply, in which she did receive, but not as promptly as she would wish. Never the less, she was all too grateful, if not entirely content, for the company.

"I'm afraid I am now, Felicity. What is it? I believe it to be night time which you are aware is for sleeping, aren't you?" *And pondering thoughts that worry our minds, dear sister,* Felicity thought to herself.

"I must talk to someone about all that has occurred in the day; I feel I will simply burst if I do not."

"You may talk, I suppose, for I am somewhat interested. They would not let me meet him, Felicity. What is he like? What is his appearance? Is he old and wrinkly with a strict demeanour, or is he young and attractive with an intense yet romantic stare?" At imagining him, Kitty found herself with a sudden abundance of energy.

"I know not his age precisely, but he seems to be twenty and something, perhaps nearing thirty. And on his appearance I have not put much thought to it, but I suppose he is attractive and pleasing to the eye if one squinted just enough." She then remembered his comments on her own appearance and felt the need to reciprocate those feelings to her sister. "On the other hand, his hair is not suitable for a man of his age, and his waistcoat was of a navy blue. – Who wears navy blue in this season? It certainly is not the fashion. And that stare of his, though it be intense, it is not romantic, I feel far too intimidated to enjoy it. But Kitty, I did not want only to talk about his appearance; I am to marry him! Oh! I do not want to marry him! Or anybody except my dear Nathaniel! Why is this world so unfair as for God to trap me so? I do everything I am expected to do, well, to the best of my ability, and I feel love, as God would have me, and yet I am punished."

"But he is so very rich, Felicity! His wealth is more than Mama had ever expected you to wed into! Imagine the size his residency will be! Perhaps it will have marble halls and tall glass windows with doors twice the height of the tallest man in Bath! Oh! And imagine the feasts you will have!"

"Feasts mean nothing to a girl in want of love, Kitty. I fear he will not be able to provide me that, despite my being sure that he will provide almost everything else. But I do not care for things as I do people. You know me, dear Kitty. I am scared to feel second to someone, and to abandon my ideals at the first opportunity presented to myself. Are you in the opinion that I should somehow opt out of this union? I am sure Mr Giles would cancel all arrangements if I protested well enough."

"Felicity! Do not waste this opportunity! For you are lucky to be offered such, and you will be too old to wed soon enough if you cage your heart so. If you will not have this man and all his wealth that comes with him – although that is not important at all – then I shall gladly volunteer to take your place. He need never know. He may well believe that he mistakenly named us." Kitty's hearty laugh was heard and appreciated well by her elder sister, yet Felicity felt that her sister was not of the opinion and advice she was searching for. Of course, she did not wish anyone to oppose her, but she did not know what her opinion was in order to oppose it as such, and confusion had rooted itself in her conscious as God's messages are rooted in the daily lives of all those who pray to him each night.

Rooted to the opinion that Kitty would be of no help, Felicity set it in her mind to pay a visit to her elder sister, Adelaide, the following day, so that she may have an answer from one whom was both experienced and trusted by her wholeheartedly. And so, with little preparation,

Felicity left their little village in the daily carriage that passed through.

The journey, although only consisting of a short forty-five minutes to travel the three miles into the neighbouring village, seemed long and painful to Felicity, who would much rather walk the distance, but time, as usual, was of the essence, and Felicity could not bear to be left by herself to put too much thought to the previous day until she was face to face and alone with her sister. She had hoped to find some conversation with the other passengers, but all three seemed too busy with keeping to themselves that the shyness within her displayed its presence, and she opted instead to stare out of the window at the countryside passing by. With not much else to pass the time, Felicity thought of nicer things, of beautiful things, attempting at one point to imagine Mr Giles with a genuine and amiable smile, yet she struggled so much so that the attempt was abandoned soon after.

"Thank you, Sir!" She called up to the cab driver as she began her short journey through the market area to the house of her sister and family. The same path had been taken by her many times over the course of the few years since Adelaide's marriage, yet somehow she had still not found the beauty in it, if there ever was any. The buildings surrounding the square were tall and dull, with no children playing in the streets, or music to be heard; the young girl could not imagine living in such a world where each day was the same as the previous one, but some unwanted feeling told her that married life would consist of this and nothing much else. This fear she forcefully struck to the back of her mind, her focus instead on the thought of seeing her sister, whom she had not had the pleasure of sharing her company

44

in some three weeks. Although to you, my dear reader, that may seem not so long at all and an easily tolerable amount of time to not see one's family, you must remember that Felicity had spent the majority of her life in the company of this one sister, and any time apart at all seemed an injustice to the friendship and trust that they had effortlessly built together. Each morning the two girls would wake, embrace each other, and spend the forthcoming day completing tasks alongside each other; they were very much inseparable, so much so that Aunt Augusta believed it lucky that Mr Nicholas Ramsey lived some three miles from Thorpe Hall, allowing them the separation they needed in order to mature and grow as women do. This separation was appreciated to a lesser estate by the younger of the two, who had no young and dashing husband to keep her mind occupied. She did however find consolation in her neighbour, Nathaniel, and so without the separation, she would never have achieved such a strong and undeniable (by all except the older women in her life) relationship. Oh! Why did her mind so often drift to him, each thought of hers carefully crafted to lead directly to his features, his sayings, his mannerisms? Still, all such follies were in the past. Now her mind must consist of being a good wife; that was all that was expected from her and there seemed no way to escape this fate.

Some minutes later, she had feebly knocked on the door of her sister's residence. A small scream of excitement was heard from within the walls, presumably from Katarina, the sound subsided a moment later, quite abruptly. A child was to be seen and not heard, they would say, as Lady Augusta strongly believed and shared publically this opinion.

"Miss Felicity," a maid answered the door, curtseying politely as she did so. "They are seated in the parlour. Katarina is much excited to see you, again." A surge of guilt plummeted through her body at forgetting the name of this young girl in her presence, perhaps younger than herself, when this girl had known her name by her countenance only? She stepped through the doorway hesitantly, and was led by the child, for that was the age group Felicity had decided she must certainly belong to, to the parlour as previously mentioned, and was delighted when her little niece bounded toward her, throwing her arms around her neck as she knelt down to receive the child.

"Tee! Tee!" The girl squealed, for Felicity is a difficult word to pronounce at such an age, and Katarina was still in the developing stages of communication by sound. Felicity kissed her meekly on the forehead, and bundled her up in her arms to join her sister and brother-in-law at the seating area.

"Ah! Felicity! It is so very nice of you to visit! I believe it has been some three weeks since you were last here?" Nicholas, for the use of first names was common between the good friends, said to their visitor, smiling as though he really were proud to be of the same family.

"Far too long, as I see it. There has been so much going on at Thorpe Hall that I have not had the time to steal away to be in your company. I shall try not to delay it as long once again," was her polite reply.

"Perhaps you will stay for dinner? We will have something special prepared for you, our much-loved guest."

"Yes, thank you. I believe I will accept your offer." All thoughts were dedicated to how one may avoid home and all that came with it now due to the previous day.

"I shall go tell the Cook. Katarina, come with daddy so your mama and auntie may converse privately as sisters do." Though the little girl made an attempt at some opposition from her being removed from the exciting circumstance of a visit from one of her favourite people, she was soon subdued with a promise of a story from the maid.

"Tell me, Felicity, what is it that troubles you so?"

"Adelaide! How on earth did you know?"

"Call it a sister's intuition, if you will, though I saw it clear as day on your countenance, particularly in the eyes. I know that something you disagree with has occurred and that you are simply in desperate need to share all, though you wish to pretend that it is not happening also."

"It is true, but perhaps I should remain silent with my worries, for most likely you would side with Mother and Aunt Augusta, and I could not bear to lose your support; knowing as much would make the circumstance seem much more intolerable."

"Felicity, I am sure I shall not disagree with whatever it is you need to say, though if I do you must understand that I say it for your benefit. I will not tell a falsehood. Now, tell me, for we may not have long before little Katarina comes bounding back in." Reluctantly, though knowing she had no other option from the moment she left for the coach earlier that day, she began to tell her tale of woe, emphasising the certain horridness Mr Giles had about his person, and making her opinion clear so that her sister may still be of the same opinion. When all had been told:

"Now that I know of the situation, I may provide my honest opinion, and I am certain you shall appreciate it, even if it is not quite what you expected."

"Oh! Adelaide! You do not mean to say that I should marry this man?" The worry in her youthful countenance was of a desperate child being told she would have to go hungry until sufficient funds could be created, yet for Felicity, her world seemed to be falling to pieces, had God no sympathy for one who prays twice daily and to a creative and romantic extent?

"Do not be so silly, Felicity! Sit back up on the sofa, there; you are no child to be begging upon your knees. No, I do not mean to say that you should marry this man entirely. You said it was your duty to marry to raise the status of our family, and in a way, yes it is. But you also have a duty to your heart, and to your writing. How would you pass the days if this Mr Giles did not allow you to put pen to paper as that is not what women do and most men would not allow such a hobby in their wife? And what of Nathaniel? Have you lost all hope so soon? You deserve to marry for love, and you were not meant for anything other than a happy marriage that is wanted on either side. Is this man really as horrid as you say, or are you simply trying to present him in his worst light so as to support your cause?"

"I suppose I was being slightly dramatic, and biased of his character, but Adelaide! You do not understand how the things he said made me feel! The words that came from his despicable mouth hurt even the blood that runs through my body! I could not bear his presence any longer, for he is not what I look for in a partner, nor an acquaintance! He is vile and horrible and arrogant and I hate him so! I do not want to be trapped with him in this union! I need someone similar to myself, although perhaps someone a little less stubborn and more intelligent. He will not suffice. I do not want to spend my entire life pondering! Oh! Adelaide! I cannot bear to think of a life where I will not be happy or free! With him I may feel as though I am in a prison of some sort. I do not do well doing what other people expect me to do when I do not like them personally. I would ruin everything we could construct between us before it even happens! Perhaps, I already have! For I have stolen myself away for the day to relay my feelings to someone I had absolute faith in their supporting me, to escape all those who disagree with me! I was not made to be a wife in this life, and God knows as much."

"Then perhaps what you mean to say is, you are scared. You are frightened of opening yourself up to new things, new places and people. You feel safe while you are surrounded by all that is familiar, and now you are faced with some new situation, that you do not quite know how to react other than to push it away. You must forget your stubbornness, Felicity, for, if you allow him, he may become your safety, you may rely on him for things you never believed you could rely on someone for. Nathaniel, although

53

you have feelings for him, is not what God has planned for you. Perhaps William is not either. But you need a reason more than being frightened of the future in order to subdue your guilty conscience. Marry him, and you will be taking a risk, but think about it from a more positive light." Felicity Thorpe listened with eagerness. "If he is wealthy, which we know he earns a considerable amount annually, then you can devote your time to your writing as he will be preoccupied. He may even assist in publishing your works, if he is of the same mind. But he cannot take such a thing away from you. You will not let him."

"If he believes I should not, then I cannot."

"Felicity, your duty to entertain the world with your works is more significant than that of marrying for the sake of acquiring some wealth. You must try to be a good wife, but not at the expense of your writing. Promise me as much, dear sister. For that is your gift to the world, given to you especially by God. Do not put it to waste due to the opinions of those around you. You have the power to write your own life."

"So, your verdict is that I must marry the Mr William Giles?"

"That is my verdict."

And so it was agreed by Felicity herself to remove all opposition on the subject from her mind and a promise was made privately to not waste this wonderful opportunity. Wonderful or not though, her sister had provided her the appreciated motivation she was in necessity of in order to please her Mother on her return, when she declared that she would happily marry William Giles. Such shock was on the woman's countenance that Felicity believed that the entertainment born from the situation was worth the little pain and reluctance she would feel in the months prior to her wedding day. Ah! The dreaded day lurking like a small, dark creature of the night in the back of her troubled mind! But it was the duty she had set her mind to and once her mind was set, she must conform. Conforming to the wants of those around her was of a different and more difficult matter on which Felicity stubbornly took pride in opposing, much to the disappointment of those in question.

"How wonderful! I told you, dear! I told you that her mind would soon change! Though, I must ask, Felicity, where on earth did you go this morning? It was not even light out when I realised your absence."

"To Adelaide's; Katarina is as mischievous as always and Mr Ramsey is in good health before you may ask." Hanging the cloak upon her hook at the door, she avoided facing her mother, for fear of satisfying her with a measly face that may have meant nothing to the girl herself, but which Mrs Thorpe would take such pleasure in assuming what it meant.

"Perhaps next time I shall go with you, for it has been a month nearly since I last saw her. We shall go together, and I would have liked to share our joyous news, but I fear you to have already done as much in such a manner that has ruined all things joyous in it."

~ Chapter Three ~

A few days had passed in silent reverie, each one bringing Felicity closer to that day, and each one causing a certain amount of excitement in the household. Unfortunately for Nathaniel, although there were of course many circumstances for which Nathaniel should be unfortunate, he had arrived to visit his dear friend on one of such days. In the parlour, both sat, their pupils catching the sight of anything other than their companion, and each sat with their hands folded together on their laps, having entered a world of formality in relation to each other, of which neither was much accustomed to nor wanted ever to be.

"I heard of your visit to your sister. I trust you had a tolerant journey and enjoyable time for the duration of your stay?"

"Very much so, thank you." And so they resumed the subsided disposition between the two of them. A few stolen glances were sent in the direction of her desired, yet he could not return them, for fear of exposing particular feelings to the one he had been forbidden to spend the remaining years of his life with. A romantic at heart, much like the girl in which is heart belonged to, he could not bear to stay away, yet he could not decide whether being faced personally with the situation was worth such pain.

"What is to become of us, Felicity?" he asked, speaking his thoughts aloud.

"Honestly, Nathaniel, I cannot tell you, for I do not know or understand. I do not wish to lose you nor do I wish to marry someone I do not know, but I must take this opportunity for my family. I owe them as much. I know of how difficult I can be at times and that perhaps such a beneficial proposal perhaps shall not be repeated."

"Dear Felicity!" His position on the sofa was abandoned as he fell to be by her side. "You do not owe anything to anyone except for yourself! As for your being difficult, you are entirely the opposite. Each day with you is much improved upon than what it would have been without your presence. You may not disagree, Felicity, for I am all too aware of the retaliation you are forming in your mind at this current moment, and I will not hear it. Instead, I propose something." Curiosity peaked momentarily in the young girl's eyes as her hands were taken by him. "Run away with me, Felicity. We may marry before they become knowledgeable on what we have done. We may live happily together for the rest of our lives."

"Nathaniel, I – I."

"You want what your heart wants, Felicity. Your mind does not have any influence over you; that is why I love you."

"You love me?" her voice faltered.

"You cannot tell? You are my entire world, Felicity. You are everything to me. I do not wish to marry you to produce heirs like Mr William Giles is doing; I am merely offering you my humble life yet my whole heart in return for yours. Do not be persuaded by those around you, for they do not take your heart nor your feelings into consideration, like I do. "

"Nathaniel, I – I do not know what to say! No, of course, I do. You cannot love me, and I cannot love you, for then this entire ordeal will present itself as more difficult than it already seems." Taking his hands in hers, she continued: "My heart longs for you, I cannot express in words how much your friendship means to myself, but we were not meant to be, and I would wish it that although we may remain friends, and I could not wish for this in particular more, but it is the best interest of both of us that you take leave from our residence for a while, only as much as is necessary, I beg you! But having you here reminds me of all I am losing and I must focus. I cannot let me family down again. I do hope you understand?"

"If that is how you feel, then I shall take my leave at once, Miss Thorpe, for I cannot sit here pretending that all is well because it is far from it. Good bye and good day." Abruptly was his manner in standing up to leave, and much anxiety was brewing on Felicity's part.

"Nathaniel! I –."

"I said good bye and good day, Miss Thorpe!" The tone in his voice frightened Felicity so much so, as never had she been witness to such a tone other than from perhaps her Aunt Augusta or mother! But coming from a man, and especially one whom she cared a great deal for, the entirety of the line shook her to her core and her mind felt as though it would never again be at ease.

On his leaving, the young Felicity sidled over to the window, watching him run from herself. How could someone be so caring and passionate and then leave in such a way that released an air of hatred?

"Felicity, there you are!" the sound of her Mother's voice, although usually causing despair, seemed so soft and gentle despite the harshness it often projected. "Your dress has arrived; I am here to do a fitting, for if you want something done properly, you must do it yourself. Felicity, are you crying?"

"I'm fine, Mother. Let's see the dress." Tears were wiped clean from her countenance before turning to face her Mother, who, on discovery, was holding a beautiful gown of white. "Oh, Mother!" The disbelief was apparent in her voice and her eyes could not remove the fabric from their field of focus. "It's beautiful. I am really to wear this?"

"Yes, of course, don't be all sentimental on me now, Felicity! Now, slip out of that so I can give you a fitting!" The slipping out was done, along with the fitting, in such a fashion that would have most usually irritated her, she enjoyed it all the more when her fingers trailed down the lace, and the fabric slipped between her fingers.

"Did he really pick this out; do you suppose?"

"He wrote in his letter that he chose it personally for you."

"He wrote a letter? Mother, why did I, his fiancé, not receive this letter first?"

"You are the subordinate here, Felicity. I am your Mother, and I wanted to read the letter and so I did."

"May I also read it?"

"It is not for such innocent eyes as yours. Now, change back into your blue dress and place this over the mannequin so as to avoid wrinkles. I trust you are capable of following such a simple instruction?"

"Yes, Mother."

So, there was a letter and this letter was not for the eyes of a young lady? Surely there could be nothing of serious consequence included, for she was almost certain it was simply her Mother taking advantage of the power she had for the little time remaining. Suppose he asked about the letter though at a later date and her eyes had not witnessed its ink?

~ Chapter Four ~

The sound of the bells singing their song had blessed Felicity's ears before, many times over the entirety of her life, yet they had never sounded as intimidating as they did now, as she walked down the aisle, flowers in hand, to a man she did not know. Regardless of the negativity that was holding a long term residency in her mind, she had no hesitancy in smiling as though William was instead Nathaniel, and forgetting the fact that within the hour she would be trapped and facing the unknown – "The unknown is the only thing worth fearing, for you may not prepare but all at the same time you may also expect anything, whether it be positive or negative, and so perhaps the unknown is the only thing you should not fear." These words had been previously said by Felicity to the only one she felt she could truly speak to without consequence, yet they did not return to her conscience in this particular moment, though if they did, perhaps this smile may have been easier to control, much like the tears forming in her eyes.

Much to her delight, however, was the knowledge that William did not consider the union worth a large amount of anything spectacular, and so consequently, the reception lasted a mere half hour in total, and the couple had found themselves in a carriage on the way to Mr Giles' estate a few miles south of the church before adequate farewells had been exchanged. "How did you like the reception, Felicity?" The sound of his voice pushing through the silence had resulted in both a physical jump and a large amount of confusion from his wife.

"It was much to my liking, thank you."

"I must warn you, Felicity, that my time at home will be limited. Work is a constant activity in my daily routine and it is important that I am not distracted. I do not mean to offend."

"You do not offend me, Sir."

"Do not call me Sir, Felicity. I am your husband now. You may call me William. If there is anything you require - anything at all – ask Mrs Farley, for she runs the household and I would like to express my hope for the two of you to find companionship with one another."

"There is one thing."

"Yes?" His eyes lingered on hers, but with an intensity she was not much used to, and the question itself she was currently forming in her mind would be of much consequence if he were to disagree.

"I would like to write. In the near future I would like to look into publishing, but for the time being, I will be in need of paper and pen." He held the contact between the eyes, but Felicity dropped her gaze for almost a second to notice a mere and hidden smile forming on his lips.

"You have a wonderful ambition, Felicity. I shall have the highest quality of both sent to you, and I believe you will find the desk in the library to be more than adequate. As for publishing, I have contacts which you will find beneficial. You must not fear to be or do anything as my wife, do you understand? You have the status to act with no consequence. All I ask is that you fulfil your wifely duties and we shall have a fond marriage." What Felicity wanted to say in response was something along the lines of: 'I am not in want of fondness, but rather love' but instead said:

"Thank you, William, of course. Are we here?" The carriage had come to a sudden halt, to which Felicity was thrown forward toward her husband slightly, who caught her with little effort or care. He opened the door of the carriage, stepped out, and turned back toward his wife after closing the door.

"I shall just be a few minutes. Wait here." No explanation followed, despite how much it was expected.

On waiting only a minute in the carriage, Felicity's curiosity and lack of patience corrupted her to leave the carriage and walk through the grounds, although she made an internal promise to remain close to the carriage so that if caught, she may use the excuse of wanting some air. What she noticed first was the quaintness of the building she could only assume her husband had entered, for it was a small cottage surrounded by countless plants which seemed

73

to have more power and beauty than the house itself. A river, in which Felicity was certain she would find most pleasing and comforting to walk along in the mornings, ran down around the side of the house, as well as her eyes which tried to follow the path it took. She wanted ever so much to walk alongside it at the current moment, but the thought that William was nearby and he had told her to stay inside the carriage, which she had already taken actions against, made her fear what his reaction may be if she had ventured further. So, instead, she closed her eyes and imagined what it led to, and the sounds of the animals she would hear, and how her feet would tiptoe softly through the soil barefoot, with her hair flying behind her in the wind –

"Felicity!" The harsh voice woke her all of a sudden from her internal creation of bliss. "I told you to stay in the carriage!" No sooner had she laid her eyes upon the man,

74

had William grabbed her by the arm and was dragging her back to the transport. "You will listen to your husband! Do you hear me?" She nodded nervously as she was thrown back into the seat and he followed her in, slamming the door shut, his eyes more intense than Felicity had ever deemed possible in a human being. "I do not want to make this difficult for you, nor for myself, but I gave you a simple instruction and you disobeyed me; you disobeyed your husband!"

"I only wanted to imagine the river." Dangerous as it was, she felt some truthful explanation was necessary. "I did not venture far from the carriage."

"I did not want you to leave the carriage at all, Felicity! You will not mention this detour to any one you find yourself conversing with, I beg of you. It was a visit of private matters, and it will stay that way, do you understand?"

"I do. You may not feel it is necessary that you must remain in conversation with myself for the duration of the journey. I am used to the silence and I quite revel in it."

"What use is a wife if I cannot talk to her?" *Many believe that is not her purpose at all* was what she thought about his statement. He confused her, much as she expected him to, for sometimes he seemed relaxed and content, and able to accept some difference in her personality, yet at other times he seemed brutal and masculine. "Tell me, why do you imagine everything?"

"What the imagination sees is often much more beautiful than the reality one is faced with."

"Perhaps it is just the responsibility of the person in question to find the beauty. Have you ever thought about it in such a way?"

"I admit I've tried to, but I feel as though as a woman I am limited as to what I am allowed to see. I am aware you will not understand what it is like to live as the weaker sex, so I will allow you to your opinion, so long as you do not disregard mine."

"Gladly, although perhaps in time I may have some influence over your opinion." His eyes now seemed a different form of intense, as now they were somewhat accepted by the receiver to an extent, and she felt a shiver travel through her skin, one which she had never experienced before. This stare was not lifted, and although Felicity felt herself becoming more uncomfortable, she felt as though she had no option to remove herself from the interaction, or if she did, the reluctance to look away for personal interest was far stronger. "Perhaps, we shall find a sort of harmony between the two of us."

"Perhaps."

"Perhaps." The repetition of her response had somehow caused shock, due to it being unexpected, much as his gaze was. What was happening, she was not aware, for this was new territory for her, and she could not make up her mind as to his character as easily as she usually could in any stranger she met. Yet he was not a stranger, for he was her husband, and she was his wife, and there seemed to be some unknown connection between the two of them, and both were waiting for the other to notice it. Neither noticed it, however, and the duration of the journey was spent in silence, although multiple glances of their partner were shared, and Felicity at one point found herself both blushing and smiling! Such was the inclination of their achieving a new stage in their relationship, but Felicity still, although not shy at heart, refused to believe that this could lead to anything more, and she would shake her head internally at her impressionable behaviour, for she owed him nothing as of yet.

"We are here." The carriage stopped and Felicity was helped out by William who offered out his hand to her, to which she accepted reluctantly and discovered the warm temperature of his skin, and how it felt both firm and comforting at the same time. A pause was taken on the touch, to which both reacted in similar ways: she looking down towards the exchange, and then towards his eyes, and him staring straight into her eyes, for he felt no inclination to deposit his field of view anywhere else.

"Thank you, William." The action of removing herself from the carriage was continued and completed, and their hands found their way back to their own body, unfortunately for Felicity though, who wanted to stay in the moment long enough to make sense of the situation.

"This is my place of residency – I should say perhaps: *our* place of residency, for it as much yours now as it is mine."

"Does it have a name?" She inquired.

"It has been labelled 'The Mansion' while in ownership of my family, but I have always felt as though the name did not match the house at all. It is not grand as it beautiful. It often reminds me of an oversized cottage, only with the architectural style of course, for there are three floors, four, including the basement." Felicity was led in the direction of the front door, and preceded up a few stone steps, only for the door to be opened to the both of them with no requirement of knocking by either of them. Mr Giles reacted little, and entered the hallway almost eagerly, although his countenance remained to some extent sour as though his only purpose was to both demonstrate and radiate the amount of power that he held. Felicity followed innocently behind him, and tried not to appear in too much awe at the room that surrounded her, for she was almost certain her mother would complain had she allowed her mouth to open in shock.

"This is Mrs Farley, Felicity." The Mrs Farley whom he was introducing was clothed in a dress and apron, but her hair was tied back in a matronly manner, and although she too seemed to express some level of power, her face seemed kinder, and Felicity found herself calmed by her presence. "She is the house keeper here, and she will show you to your rooms."

"Shall I not be staying with you?"

"For the time being I believe you will benefit from some privacy while you settle down in such a new life. Besides, I am rarely home and I would not wish to disturb you." Seeing no adequate reason to argue or question further, Felicity smiled at the housekeeper, who returned a beautiful one as Felicity believed she would have, and Felicity was led to the rooms in question.

~ Chapter Five ~

On remaining in the room in which she was guided to only a few hours earlier, Felicity had studied each part hidden within those four walls, and even some of that which was to be seen from the windows, for fear of spending the night in a new place was heavy on her mind, most particularly due to the knowledge that she would be alone. Of course, sleeping next to a strange man, whom she felt did not like her to a large extent as of yet, did not quite appeal to her either, yet she believed that knowing she was not alone would help contain some of that fear. She felt in her heart quite strongly that if she was able to familiarise herself with the room, then a warm feeling of content would rest inside her, and she wouldn't feel quite so lost.

A knock came at the door.

"Come in," Felicity faltered, standing as straight as she could make herself with her hands in front of her.

"It's just me, Mrs Farley. Thought I'd help you get ready for the dinner." She closed the door behind her quietly and made her way to the tall mahogany wardrobe, while Felicity found that she was unable to move.

"Excuse me, Mrs Farley. Did you say *the* dinner?"

"Did he not tell you?" Her curiosity was answered with a confused shake of the head by the young girl, to which Mrs Farley shook her own. "We are to have guests tonight; two in fact, from Germany. The old gentleman is Mr Marmaduke Zweiful, and I believe he will be attending with his daughter, who, if I remember correctly, is called Frieda."

"Why would Mr Giles be receiving guests from Germany?"

"Mr Zweiful was in business with Mr Giles' Father many years ago, and consequently Mr Giles was allowed to accompany his father on many of their business trips to Germany where I believed he kept a close acquaintance with Frieda. She was never much over here though, I'll tell you that, and she keeps to herself, very quiet and meek, more so than you. Hold this for me, dear. All you must know is that Mr Zweiful is a very powerful man and you must behave so. Try if you find it possible to have some light conversation with the daughter, though I would not blame you if you found it too challenging for I myself I have not dared to. It is not that she is of a rude or negative nature, mark me, but more so that I feel I would run out of things to say to a child who never replied, and I am not usually one to find myself speechless."

"How old is Frieda?"

"I couldn't say for certain, although I would estimate that she is around your age. Perhaps that will bring the young girl some comfort, and maybe after all these years I will finally witness the child talk! Ha! Imagine that!" While the conversation on the extraordinary visitors from Germany continued, Felicity was helped into a beautiful dress of white organdie with a blue sash. Looking in the mirror afterwards, Felicity was revealed to someone not like herself, or at least, who she used to be, but now a Lady, of status, with a husband and wealth.

"You look beautiful. God Forbid Mr Giles might actually notice you tonight."

"Is that to say he may not?"

Mrs Farley stumbled to place her words together before answering. "I meant nothing by it. Do forgive me." But the art of forgiving was not to be practised, for Mrs Farley

86

left the room at an unimaginable and suspicious pace and Felicity was left to herself once again.

The dinner that had been previously mentioned soon came around and Felicity found herself nervous beyond compare. The guests that Mrs Farley had warned her off in such detail yet also without any, arrived in such a style that almost matched Mr Giles, for their carriage was one of the grandest Felicity had imagined one to be, and both were clothed in such elegant clothing that she felt underdressed in her organdie; she told herself that such matters had never bothered her previously, and that the dress she wore currently was much more suited to herself personally than a gown as grand as Miss Zweiful's would.

"Ah! Mr Zweiful, welcome, do come in! Miss Zweiful, it is lovely to see you again. How are you? Good, good! May I introduce you both to my new wife, Mrs Felicity Giles, formerly Miss Thorpe, of Thorpe Hall. I am sure you will not have heard of it, for it is not large, but it certainly is one of the most beautiful little homes I have ever laid eyes upon. Perhaps you will have the pleasure of visiting it one day in the near future, although I know you are rarely away from Germany. Do; come in to the dining room, just this way!"

The look exchanged between Mr Giles and Miss Zweiful was very much noticed by Felicity, who reacted little physically, yet inside, her heart pounded a little, as though she was jealous of the attention he had given their guest. Only a look was in question, a simple shared glance, yet Felicity felt it to be much more. Perhaps it was in relation to her previous conversation with Mrs Farley, whom had suggested something involving the two beings in front of her, and she felt herself beginning to assume something had happened; what that was, though, she was not certain.

The three were escorted into the dining room by Mr Giles, who personally tucked Miss Zweiful and chair under the table for her, and Felicity was left to the same treatment by one of the servants. She whispered her thanks, yet she secretly wished that her husband had completed the task.

"How long are you both to be staying in England?" Mr Giles questioned.

"Only a fortnight, for England is not quite as satisfying as Germany. The weather is usually atrocious, if I may say so."

"You may, Sir, for you speak nothing but the unfortunate truth."

The two men spoke of business and other such boring subjects that Felicity felt no danger of being spoken to, and used the time to take occasional glances at the girl sat opposite her. Mrs Farley had been right in saying she was of a similar age, for she really did seem to be only perhaps fifteen or sixteen. Her hair was of a golden colour, with each curl more perfect than the last, and her eyes an ocean blue, her skin smooth-seeming, and her mannerisms were that of a lady, so much so that Felicity was almost certain that this girl was the embodiment of what her own Mother expected of herself. Felicity would never be like Miss Zweiful, she feared.

"How long have the two of you been married, Mrs Giles?" The question from Miss Zweiful had caught Felicity very much in surprise, and she took a moment to compose herself before answering.

"Please, call me Felicity."

"Then I insist you call me Frieda."

"Of course, Frieda. We were married only this morning." The shock on her face matched that of which resided in Felicity at the conversation beginning. "It has all happened at such a quick pace, I must admit."

"Yes, I feel as though my father and I are intruding now." She leaned in, whispering so that the men not be subject to their topic of conversation.

"At first I was reluctant, but now I see you are of a kind nature, and I do not know Mr Giles as well as one may wish to know their husband, and so I must thank you for your company, and for beginning the conversation. I was persuaded you were not interested in conversing with myself."

"Oh! Of course I am! I just can be shy at times, I do apologise if I made you nervous at all in the silence." The two young girls conversed pleasantly for the duration of the meal, while the two men did the same, each set keeping separate to the other, as it should be. Despite earlier

91

suspicions of Frieda and her husband, all had ceased to exist having learned more of her acquaintance's character, and Felicity found herself wishing that the two would perhaps stay longer than two weeks in England.

"Oh, look at the time!" This declaration from Mr Zweiful caught the attention from the entire party, and, despite earlier thoughts, Felicity wished he was simply expressing his shock at the time, and not implying anything further. "Frieda and I must be going. I thank you for the dinner, Mr Giles, and I hope to see you again before we return to Germany. Auf Wiedersehen, the both of you." He rose from the table, Frieda following neatly by his side as they headed towards the front door. The girls said their goodbyes, and Felicity hesiated down the hall, out of sight, where she believed Mr Giles would rather she be, and she watched as the old man left first, and how her husband and new friend hovered in front of eachother, Frieda seeming unsure how to react. Though, of course, Mr Giles seemed to know exactly how to enact the farewell, and he kissed Frieda, holding onto her with his arm wrapped aorund her lower back – *how could he?* Felicity thought. He had barely touched her at all other than to help her down from the carriage and before that to physciaslly drag her back to the carriage – yet here he was with the girl whom Mrs Farley had her suspicions about, kissing her in the doorway, unaware of Felicity's distant presence.

She turned on her heels almost directly, reluctant to watch such a show any longer, and spent the entirety of the evening alone in her new room, the quiet and loneliness suffocating her, until she found herself crying into her new pillows.

~ Chapter Six ~

Two days had passed since Felicity had witnessed the confusing event, and those two days had passed with neither Mr or Mrs Giles addressing or conversing with the other, for William had no knowledge that Felicity knew of his secret affair, and Felicity did not understand what she had seen; she was only a young girl still after all, and William was a grown man. Both sat to eat their meals at the same table, but still, no words were communicated. Felicity noticed early on that he did not even look in her direction, although it was not as though she either expected him to or wanted him to. However, I can assure you, dear reader, that he did in fact look in her direction, most specifically towards herself, where he found himself able to spend hours analysing her dainty features and never becoming bored, yet he would look away whenever her eyes wandered a little too close to himself; he could not risk seeming less important than what he was, of course. This behaviour lasted two days, as I previously mentioned, and then, on the third day, Felicity was prepared, although reluctantly, to continue doing so, yet when she arrived in the dining room for breakfast he was not there, nor was his newspaper on the table waiting for him. Perhaps he was late? No, he was as punctual as one could be, extraordinarily so.

"Mrs Farley, may I inquire where Mr Giles is this morning?"

"He left early hours this morning, dear. Thought he would have told you?"

"He has told me nothing since the Zweiful's were here; not even a word."

"You're both as stubborn as each other. He won't be returning for a few days, mind you, but when he returns, try and spark some conversation, dear; after all, he is your husband." Felicity nodded in reply and resumed her seat at the large table by herself. Never had she dined alone in the past, for she had many sisters. Solitude was not something she had acclimated to in her short life, yet she feared that William was not a stranger to mysteriously disappearing without a warning of any sort, and that being alone would be something she would have to grow used to. This was followed by a larger fear, however, which was that William had married her for a reason, a practical reason, which was to produce an heir. Although it had never been so much as mentioned between the two of them, neither had anything else, and something would happen soon; how soon, Felicity did not know, and she had assumed that by now the wedding would have already been consummated, yet he was in no rush to do such a thing.

The breakfast was eaten, however, with some reluctance from Felicity, yet she found the freedom to walk through the house with the knowledge that she could do nothing wrong while William was not home to be quite satisfying and relieving. She found that she could explore rooms she had been too scared to venture in before under his presence. Yet this freedom was short-lived, for, as she sat in one of the sitting rooms, Mrs Farley let herself in.

"Someone here for you, Ma'am. Should I show them in?" Felicity nodded her head nervously, wondering who it could possibly be.

"Adelaide!" The shock of her sister's arrival and presence by the doorway was enough excitement to cause Felicity to run from her seat to embrace her sister in such a hug that Adelaide had been reminded of how young she really was. "You did not tell me you would be visiting! Come, sit with me!" Felicity grabbed her sister by the hand. "How have you been? How is Katarina?"

"We are all fine, thank you, but I came here to see how you were doing, there has been so much happen in so little time that I am worried about your state of mind. Marrying someone you love and are content with is one thing, a much more beautiful thing, but you have been forced into this, and I worry that you may not cope. I know how headstrong you can be, but now that you have committed yourself to this man, you must be the best wife that you can be."

"You say these things as if this was your opinion of it all along, yet I remember all too clearly the conversation in which you told me that my only duty was to myself and my

99

writing. Which is it that I am supposed to dedicate myself to? Surely I cannot do both, for however much William seemed to approve of my hobby prior to our engagement, that may not be how he really feels on the matter. I could not bear it if he were to not allow me to follow my dream, am I to just stay home and play wife? I was not meant for this."

"Of course you were not. You were always meant to be a writer, and to fall in love, for that is all that you deserve. You must remember the limited time you have had together, and you must create more of that time, and perhaps your dreams will coexist at one point."

"You mean to say I may fall in love with William?" Thoughts of what she had witnessed only a day before seemed to block the idea of this, how could she ever love someone whose heart belonged to someone else? Despite this, the realization that Felicity was also in love with someone else became apparent in her mind, and she felt almost guilty for the following second at the thought. "There is something I must tell you, but you must promise that you will never tell another living soul."

"Of course, now what is it, dear sister?"

"I think that William may be having an affair with a young German girl of the name Frieda Zweiful."

"And tell me, why do you think this?" Even though she seemed to be questioning Felicity, doubtfulness abundant, her eyes instead showed fear and worry, as if they knew that there was in fact no doubt in the subject.

"Mrs Farley told me of the rumours before she and her father dined with us, and then, upon leaving, William was escorting her out and they embraced each other. It was horrible to watch, Adelaide! And now he has left, and may not return for a few days! Perhaps he has gone to stay with the Zweiful's?"

"If there are rumours, then it suggests to me that this is a thing of the past, and that these rumours will soon be put to the rest now that he is married – to you, may I remind you? Perhaps he has travelled to visit their residence so that he may end the affair. It is not uncommon among men to do so, and so you must expect it, but from what I know of William, he would not hurt you."

"I'm sorry to disturb you, Mrs Giles, but you have another visitor: Mr Edmunds. He would like to speak with you alone." At this, a worried glance was exchanged between the two girls, one which caused suspicion and curiosity from the housekeeper as to who this man was in relation to them.

"You may send him in," she directed towards her new friend, and then, upon turning to her sister, as Nathaniel stood by the door. "I thank you for visiting me. Please do visit again soon, for I get terribly lonesome in this house all by myself, and I would very much appreciate your company."

"Of course I shall, as soon to this date as is possible, I promise you. Do be careful with Nathaniel. You are lucky that William is not around to witness this as you were for him." A warm embrace was shared between the sisters before she left the room, only to be replaced by another figure from a past that seemed to be a lifetime ago.

"Felicity," the one word which had left his lips thousands of times before came out nearly incomplete, his voice struggling with nerves which he did not expect. He stood awkwardly by the door, his hands by his side, dropped from a sturdy, masculine position of power behind his back. For a moment, Felicity followed a similar pattern of losing all body strength and wanting to embrace him once more, but her sister's words were stronger.

"Nathaniel, you cannot come here anymore. It is too difficult to be reminded of what I couldn't have but almost did. The only possible way to move on from this situation is to do just that; create distance." Believing bluntness to be the safest and easiest option, Felicity set her opinion straight, allowing him only a moment to process her words before continuing. "You must know how much I hate to say such a thing, for I admire you dearly, Nathaniel, but now that I am married, I have a duty to William."

"I understand. I have fooled myself for the past few weeks into thinking that we could be something more still, and that we would somehow find a way like we always seem to do. Must we split completely though? Cannot we be friends?"

"Not now, no. We must put distance first." She stood up slowly, and walked towards him, trying to hold back tears which she was so used to having when thinking of him, and embraced him one last time, holding him in the hug longer as she felt his strong arms wrap around her back.

"You must be Nathaniel." His stern, low voice echoed from behind Nathaniel, Felicity face to face with him as they pulled apart.

"William, you're back already?" Felicity's voice now faltered as Nathaniel's had done only minutes ago.

"I only went for some short business, yet I return to find my wife embracing another man. I was warned of you by her Mother. Since you are here I would like to take the opportunity to tell you that you are not welcome here, nor anywhere in close proximity to my wife for the matter. I hope, as I have asked this request of you in such a polite manner, that you will kindly leave and respect this."

"What right have you to remove myself from Felicity's life? You do not deserve such a girl as her, and I shall not leave until I am ready to do so, good sir!" Within only a short moment, William's eyes became more intense than usual, radiating some terror that he would soon inflict upon the man if he did; Felicity even thought she saw his fists clenching.

"Nathaniel, just leave, please. Remember what I said." He looked towards her eyes in the hope that he wasn't taking her husband's opinion, but there was nothing there except fear and urgency. William, however, could not hold himself any longer, and he grabbed Nathaniel by the arm, pulling him in the direction of the front door; the entire scene caused Felicity's skin to prick, and she watched in fear, paralyzed to the spot.

~ Chapter Seven ~

The days passed in perfect bliss, or in as much bliss as could be expected, for William and Felicity still resumed their relationship and skill of avoiding conversation with one another, excepting a 'good morning' when they sat at the breakfast table, but neither seemed ready to converse further as of yet. Felicity felt some feeling towards him that she had not experienced in relation to her husband, but the feeling was indeed new altogether so much so that her young and innocent heart did not know exactly what the feeling was or meant.

Instead of allowing herself to worry over this circumstance, or imply importance on the matter, Felicity spent the majority of her time alone in the library, either immersing herself in some fine piece of literature, or enjoying time writing some fictional story. These stories she produced were in fact a set of short stories she kept confidential, locked in a drawer in her new room, for the matter did not seem to her important enough to mention to Mrs Farley, who she felt was nothing more than an acquaintance at the current time, and for most obvious reasons, she would not venture to even want to show her husband; William was still too much of an unknown to let him read her private writing, or into her deepest thoughts

Such was the current occupation of her time, in that she sat concentrating over one of the many desks in abundant supply around the household, writing with parchment and pen in hand, each word released contributing toward distracting her from each misery and hardship that seemed to pass. Here she found temporary solace, and she was always grateful for the time alone, for it felt much like the time before; for there was a time before, and there was a time she saw as after, split through the centre distinctly. Words seemed even more to act in place of an escape, to escape the wifely duties she now possessed, and the husband who confused her terribly to the extent she feared that she was always doing something wrong: what other reason could there be for such silence? And so, pen in hand, she allowed the words to flow, ink to paper, daily, for as many hours as she could spare in the days. For this she was grateful of her absent husband.

"Ah, Felicity, I did not know you were here," due to the silence of the past weeks, his voice toward the entryway of the library caught her by surprise.

"I can leave if you would like me to," was the meek reply she gave as she collected the countless sheets of paper she had filled for her current story, but in the rush and shock of the situation, the sheets were dropped onto the floor, their order ceasing to exist no more. William ran towards the commotion, falling to his knees to assist, the papers rescued by his masculine hands. Felicity too had lowered herself to participate in the same act, and, consequently, skin touched skin as the two paralysed themselves in their current position, each one aware of the boundary they had crossed which had been held so strictly in place since their wedding.

"I, er –," began Mr Giles.

"I do apologise, thank you for your assistance, but I will leave you to your work now." The papers were collected from William's grip as they had been collected from the pile on the floor, but something overcame the man, for on seeing Felicity resume a standing position and begin to leave his company, he too rose and grabbed her – though softly I should point out, for at heart he had a gentle and loving mind – by the arm, holding her back.

"Actually, I would prefer it if you would stay," he managed to say, while Felicity glanced at her arm held high in the air due to this height.

"I would just be in your way." She blushed at the ground, the one feminine thing she seemed capable of doing naturally, and felt his gaze on her.

"Not at all. With your permission, I would very much like to read the fiction on those pages." Felicity's face must have demonstrated to a clear extent as to how she felt about the circumstance, for William dropped her arm, and took a step back. "I did not mean to offend. I am merely curious as to what you spend all these hours in here immersing yourself in. You are rarely elsewhere in the house, which I find odd for not only is there countless rooms, but there are three libraries, yet your days are spent entirely here."

"The light shines much brighter at this side of the house, and the humble size of this particular library reminds me of home." As the words escaped her lips, she realised all too late how easily she had opened up to him.

"I like the way you think."

"You do not know how I think. You do not know me." This was not said in a spiteful way to prove that their distance was very much appreciated on this side, but to convey the opposite: I want you to know me.

"And I fear that you do not know my real character, you have only been witness to my temper, and ability to socialise with anyone but you. We have been blessed by God with the time to learn these things, however, and I would like you to know that although I may be distant, that is simply the nature I have allowed myself to become, and as my wife, I leave it your responsibility to change such a thing. May I trust you on the situation?"

"You may, although I hope you are aware that friendships are formed by effort from both parties?"

"You are already teaching me so much, little bird. I shall be an expert husband in no time with your assistance, I am sure of it." His smile seemed contagious, so much so that Felicity smiled in response, unable to hold a straight face, or refrain from blushing. Surely this much blushing would be considered unladylike?

The following day, this progression had been placed in a dangerous situation, for Nathaniel Edwards – who, as you may remember from previously, was refused the right of visitation to the Giles' residence – did in fact invite himself round, much to the surprise of Felicity when she was taking a stroll in the garden alone to see such a figure from her past who had been told to remain firmly in that past.

"Nathaniel! What on earth possessed you to return? You must leave at once!" Physical distance was instantly created between the two of them, as felicity positioned herself around the other side of a flower patch surrounding a fountain; she did not dare risk exposure.

"Surely you did not expect that I would remain in our village waiting to hear news of you?" Unsure of how to respond, Felicity hesitated, pleading him with her eyes to continue so that she may escape the responsibility of forming a reply that was worthy and coherent. Fortunately, he did so, but with an undesirable outcome. "You told me to stay away, but you do not see how my heart yearns for yours, or how I cannot live through the time it takes for the moon to orbit our home without my mind wandering to thoughts of you. Felicity," the word hung on his lips more so than she was comfortable with, for every second she felt more as though she was betraying William, every word a mockery of his very person. Yet, she felt reluctantly compelled to stay, to hear what he was really feeling, for feelings were something that William could not contribute to the development of their relationship, and here was Nathaniel offering as much, and of course, she could reciprocate those feelings. Despite these facts, however, the want to reciprocate was absent, and all thoughts were with William, most particularly their encounter in the library previously. "Run away with me and let us forget this miserable life."

"I do hope you are not serious in your proposition! Nathaniel, I am no longer yours, and I am reluctant to say that I no longer wish to be. I am happy now." Difficult though it was, the words were necessary to be said, and they must be said with such force and meaning that the receiver could not doubt their message. "Nathaniel, as my husband previously mentioned, you are no longer welcome here and I would appreciate it if you would leave immediately."

"Surely you cannot mean such a thing, dear Felicity?"

"I'm sure she means every word of it." Behind Felicity came the footsteps of William, his timing both impeccable, if not terrifying for his wife, until she realised what he had said; he understood that she felt the words, at least to some extent. "I asked politely before, but if you wish to leave in a more difficult and embarrassing way – well, that too can be arranged."

"Good day, to the both of you. I shall not return again, I can see clearly that I am wasting my time here." The two men exchanged one such look that left goose bumps on Felicity's arms, and shock in her countenance. Nathaniel did not hold this stance for a long moment, and he turned on his heels with an angry physicality, not even turning around for one last look at what he had always believed to be his future, but, if he had, he would have seen Felicity in William's arms.

"Thank you, William. I did not tell him to come here again; I want you to know that."

"That is alright; he will not bother us again. Now, how would you feel about accompanying me for a walk through the garden?"

~ Chapter Eight ~

A week had passed almost expeditiously, and the times spent between wife and husband increased much compared to those first few weeks of reluctant marriage. Walks in the garden were plenty, and William's proposition to read Felicity's writing was finally accepted after just three days of their new friendship, but the union still had yet to be consummated, but both party accepted that this would come in time, when the two of them were ready. Communication also proved to be a strength between the couple, and Felicity found herself enjoying the company of William, so much so that all those moments where she found herself in solitude, only thoughts of him wandered through her girlish mind. Despite this series of blissful days, a figure from her past still returned on the daily to torment her on her decision, yet he was denied access to the house, and Felicity would be forced to endure knowing he was on the other side of the wall as she glanced aimlessly out of the window every few moments; his presence was not so easily forgotten due to their long and beautiful history.

Upon one of such days was access somehow successful on Nathaniel's part and he found Felicity within minutes of wandering the halls, thrusting doors open in such a violent manner that all the servants were consumed by too much fear to remove him from the premises, despite the very clear orders they had received from their master on the matter.

"Felicity!" On arriving in the room in which his ambition was currently within, he strode over to the girl, his fingers locking around her wrist.

"Nathaniel! I beg of you, let me go!" She squirmed painfully under his restriction, but no attempt would delay his decision to leave the residence in such a way. "Someone! I need assistance!" Her voice echoed down the halls and initially her requests were met only with concerned stares from the staff, until her husband rushed down the hall – very masculine although not very civilised – and reacted with such violence that was reciprocated from the trespasser.

The entirety of the situation passed almost in seconds, and Felicity stood only a few feet away in bewilderment, confusion and relief all at once. But within minutes, Nathaniel had been escorted from the land with the addition of multiple bruises and a dent to his reputation. William had emerged from the fight with similar repercussions, yet this particular side to him had been known by the staff, but not by Felicity who stood alone, unsure quite how to respond to the situation. On the one hand, he had protected her, although that was only part of his duties as a husband, but he had looked toward her afterwards, fear on his face, but not from the prior event itself, but rather more so that he had showed more of himself, and he was frightened of how he would now be perceived by his new friend. So much had developed between the two of them recently and he could not bear to believe that it had been wasted.

"I suppose I should thank you, William. I did not ask him here, I promise you. I would not do that to you." Felicity stated, upon fearing silence between the two of them again, much like the introductory weeks of their marriage.

"No thanks are required, Felicity. You were in need of help, and it is partly my fault that such a divide has been forced between the two of you, although I must admit that I feel a lot better about such an act now that his true self has been revealed. I would not want you to be hurt. Perhaps," he began, leaving parted lips for just a moment, creating such a tension between them that Felicity found herself looking at his lips. "- you shall not think of me too differently. I am afraid I acted in a way that is not civilised, and I fear I frightened you."

"I do think of you differently, but not in the way you may be thinking, for you demonstrated, although I must admit I was rather frightened, that you are loyal and protective, both of which are such masculine traits that I shall like you all the more for."

"Then I suppose I should thank Nathaniel for allowing me to demonstrate such traits?" he laughed, the tension minimised again. "You are so quiet at times, Felicity, yet at other times I overhear you talking with the servants, or your sister, and you speak for everyone in the room. Perhaps it is merely my presence in the room which causes you to subdue your thoughts?"

"I am always told that I talk far too much for anyone's liking. There is much to say, no matter who may be in the room, but while around you I try much harder to be a good wife, and a good person. I do not mean to offend."

"You do not offend purposefully, Felicity. But I enjoy listening to you. Your voice is beautiful and soft like a girl's should be, and when accompanied by your inner most thoughts, I can imagine it to be the most beautiful thing to be heard by any man."

"Thank you." Felicity began, unsure as to what to say; this did not occur all too often, but all she was in want of at the current moment was to write. "And thank you again for helping with..."

"Yes, of course, no problem at all!" Upon this, Felicity smiled nervously, and turned slowly, taking a few steps down the path back towards the house.

"Are you returning to the library? I can escort you back."

"Yes, but I can go myself, if that is okay with you? I think I shall write for a while."

"Of course, I shall leave you to your writing then. Have a good day, Felicity."

As decided previously, Felicity had spent the remainder of the day and the evening writing at a desk in the smaller of the libraries – here she felt like she would be disturbed less and that she wouldn't be in the way to the same extent she would be in one of the main libraries. Pages upon pages were written and an ink pot of jet black ink fully used, and when the clock downstairs had struck 12,

127

a short story of the life of a young girl had been produced. Pride and satisfaction filled Felicity's mind, along with the shock that she had been able to ignore the events of the day, or at least use them to create literature. She had laid out the pages in a pile on the desk in front of her upon completion, and allowed herself a minute to run her fingers over the paper; it had been so long since her writing had caused her to feel such a way; it was a relief, a freedom, an escape. But her happiness was interrupted when a knock came at the library door.

"Mrs Giles, there is a letter for you."

"Thank you," Felicity received the envelope and the servant left the room, allowing her to be once again in silence and solitude. On opening the letter, she was first filled with excitement when she realised that it had come from her father, but the first line filled her entirely with dread and hatred.

My dearest Felicity,

I am unable to express how I am capable of writing such a thing to you in writing, for I feel as though it is my duty as your father and human being to emit to you such news to your face directly. Yet I am also unable to leave the residence, and I fear that we do not have much time left. Phyllis has fallen ill; even the Doctor is uncertain about what it could possibly be. I do not wish to worry you, and I apologise for the abruptness of the letter, but I would advise you to return home for a while, for Phyllis may not have much time left with us and she has been calling for you ever since this dreadful thing occurred.

Sincerely,

Your father.

On finishing the letter, Felicity was filled with such urgency that the manuscript was altogether forgotten about. She rushed from the desk, then the room, and ran through the hallways, trying to find her husband. After only a moment of searching, he was discovered in the larger library of the three, and on rushing into the room, Felicity faltered on seeing his face.

"Felicity, what is the matter? What is wrong?" He placed his book down on the nearest shelf, clearly not caring that it had not been placed correctly, and raced towards his wife, holding her hands within his, and looking deeply into her eyes from one to the other.

"It is Phyllis! Father has written me a letter explaining the whole ordeal! I must return home immediately!"

"Of course! How long shall you be gone for?" Although there was a large amount of energy between them both, his tone became serious quite quickly.

"I cannot promise a time or a date, but I have to be there for her; she is my sister." William understood all too well what must be done.

And so, a bag was packed for Felicity, and she took one of her new carriages home, the familiarity unwelcome.

~ Chapter Nine ~

Felicity had only been present in the household home for three days before Phyllis had passed. The girls, including Adelaide who had visited also, had all tried their hardest to raise her spirits by putting on puppet shows, playing musical pieces, and Felicity even wrote her a poem. All had been present when the time had come, when the wind outside seemed to still, and the curtains no longer flowed through the wind, and her presence was no longer felt, as her eyelids slowly fell over her eyes that had once been more alive than those of her sisters.

Adelaide had left only the day after, hoping that an expedient return to her usual life would work as an appreciated distraction from the hardships the family had endured over the previous week, where an illness had appeared seemingly from nowhere in particular, and death had stolen their sweet, little sister.

Felicity stayed one more day after this, but found that the darkness that now seemed to haunt the house was too much, and a letter had been sent to her new home requesting a carriage to arrive for 4 o'clock that day.

"Return home soon, Felicity. Happiness and brightness is at a loss here, and I can find it in you." Her father told her as she climbed gracefully into the carriage.

"I will, Father. Although I do not feel the same as I did before I came here. There is no more happiness or brightness left in my heart anymore, and I fear there shan't be for a long time; not until this hole in my chest heals." Felicity could not see it in his eyes, and consequently she would never know, but her Father felt himself grieving for more than just Phyllis; Felicity had changed from this experience, and it appeared that it would be a permanent state. He could not bear it if his daughter had refused to acknowledge the creativity and imagination within her mind, when she was capable of so much more than he had been, and she had always been known to have such a high energy; even though Lady Augusta had disapproved. Her opinion seemed to matter less, for due to Felicity being married and Phyllis' sudden death, there was only poor Kitty's future left to decide, and so Lady Augusta had made it up in her mind to return within a couple of years to find her someone suitable to settle down this, but for now, she was not needed.

So, Felicity had returned home in the carriage, which usually was as comfortable as carriages came, but now she felt trapped within the walls, and the window had to be kept open to allow air in until the cold evening air became unbearable. The coldness remained when she arrived, and even when William helped her down from the carriage and enquired after how she was feeling and any news of Phyllis. On seeing the tears that were formed at the mention of her name, however, he had come to a speedy judgement and decided it best not to mention anything unless Felicity seemed open to it. However, when Felicity ignored the rest of his enquiries and concerns, he became worried, and allowed her to enter the house before gripping her shoulders, forcing her to face him. No words were capable of being spoken, however, and instead Felicity found herself in tears, falling into her husband's chest, which he responded to by wrapping his arms tightly around her petite figure. No words were said for the remainder of the moment, for just being held by his strong arms was all she needed for while at home, she had been in a state of shock, and knowing that she must pretend to be coping with the circumstance so as not to upset her Mother even more, who had spent more time crying over Phyllis than not; as much was expected from the sensitive woman though, for her four girls meant more to her than just marriage prospects for rich young men deep in her heart – very deep indeed. After the moment was finished, Felicity pulled herself from his grip slowly, wiped her tears, and looked him in the eye for only a second before turning to climb the staircase to her chamber. William was not at the same stage, however, and once again like the many times before, he gripped onto her small hand, forcing her to turn back to him.

"I would like to invite your family round to dinner tomorrow night, and I would like to ask your permission to do so."

"Oh, yes; I am sure they would greatly appreciate that. Thank you." Although it was apparent they both had nothing more to say on the subject, neither had made an effort to move, and Felicity's hand was still held by his. He looked into her eyes, the moment lasting forever yet passing by quickly at the same time as his other hand hesitantly moved to caress her cheek. Unsure what else to do, Felicity allowed him to continue; never had she been so close to any man before, not even Nathaniel, and his presence was so apparent to her all at once, but she found herself leaning closer towards his lips. As she did so, he did the same, tilting her face softly. The embrace became a kiss; simple and quick, but at the same time, it was not rushed to any extent and had been a pleasant occurrence for both of them. Still holding on to her head, they both pulled away and William left it only seconds before enquiring:

"I would very much like for you to stay with me tonight." The words came ever so beautifully from the lips she had just kissed, and her attention was still upon them. Although this was a new experience, she had felt it to be right, and that he was right.

"I would like that very much," she paused before an addition to her answer which caused goose bumps to find residence on his skin. "William."

~ Chapter Ten ~

"Thank you ever so much for inviting us round for dinner, Mr Giles! I cannot thank you enough for providing us such a beautiful distraction on behalf of our daughter! She has been gone far too long already but God will be protecting her in heaven, I should hope so, for she was the most well-behaved child who would have had ownership of such a bright future – or at least with her beauty and such things she would have secured herself a good husband and consequently an improved status upon what little we have! Oh, my dear, dear Phyllis! I cannot bear to be apart from her! I wish I could be with her, to comfort her, and tell her that all will be well again!" Mrs Thorpe had a way of talking rather too much, despite all the times she had warned

Felicity off doing such a thing herself; yet she did not see her hypocritical ways in which she governed her daughters.

"Phyllis seems to have been a wonderful girl with a wonderful life. She was lucky to have you as a Mother," William replied, putting a hand on his Mother in-law's arm to comfort her. Felicity sat at the other side of her Mother, looking towards her husband at any chance that became available to her. The night between the two of them had been special, and had developed their relationship even further as a clear display of trust had been provided on both sides. Felicity finally felt comfortable with him, and William was proud that he had managed to protect Felicity in such a way that she had fallen in love with him; for that was what it was: love.

"Dear William, you are such a gentleman. My Felicity is lucky to have you, indeed." The tears streamed down her face in such a fashion that they were joined by cries and sobs, so loud that Felicity fetched her a glass of water.

"May I excuse myself and Felicity for just a few minutes? We shall not keep you long." William's question had caught his wife by surprise, for Felicity was unaware of any reason for their absence to be required.

"Of course, dears! Hopefully I shall have composed myself upon your return! Ah! Katarina! Put that down, dear! That is not to be played with!"

William took Felicity by the hand and led her out of the room and into the smaller library.

"Dear William, why have you brought us to the library?" The door was shut quietly behind her, and William strode up the desk, unlocking the top drawer and pulling out

Felicity's manuscript; it was the one written the night she had received news of her dear sister. "My manuscript?"

"Yes. I hope you do not mind but I took pleasure in reading it while you were visiting home. It is simply wonderful, Felicity, from the plot to the characters. I enjoyed it thoroughly. I have plans to send it to a publisher in the town in which I work; even under your name if they believe it will sell well. Don't just stand there, Felicity, tell me what you think!" He had a look on his face that implied pride and excitement but Felicity did not know what to think; shock was the most prominent, along with excitement too but this was preceded by worry that he may not have enjoyed it, even though he had just told her so in many ways.

"William, I cannot believe you would do such a thing for me. I never more than dreamed of being published, for I am a woman. It is not expected."

"Then together we shall make it expected! Society has brought together these silly ideals that completely disregard all individuality one may possess. They think of nothing but money and status, much as your mother, if I may be so brave as to point out, yet they think nothing of talent. Yours shall be a name known by all, from our small little town to the bustling streets of London. Imagine, Felicity, think of your book owned by all the wealthy families of our time! I am proud to call you my wife; I knew of your gift when I met you for I could see it in your eyes what you held in your heart most dearly. We have a meeting with my friend Tuesday coming - say you'll accept!"

"Oh, William! Of course I accept, for I would be silly not to!"

"Then I suppose you would like to return to your family and tell them of the good news?"

"Rather would I keep it between ourselves for a time - for my Mother is already distressed with dear Phyllis, if I were to tell her I was to be an authoress, well, I fear I may cause her death." William laughed heartily to this, and returned the manuscript to its rightful place in the drawer before taking his wife's hand. They returned to the dining room, where the family had situated themselves upon Mrs Farley's request, for the food had been prepared and was ready for serving. Both husband and wife took their place at each end of the mahogany table, the remaining source of light for the day shining joyfully through the dominating windows onto the china plates and mourning family. A pianist in the adjoining room had been hired to play Phyllis' most enjoyed music.

"Phyllis would have loved this ever so much! I can just imagine her excitable reaction to the piano, and this

146

grand food in such a grand house. I thank God for the safety

of the three other girls, and now my son! God has blessed

us, and Phyllis, I am sure, will be content in heaven!" Mrs

Thorpe cried to the table, trying to smile through the tears.

"Ah! The food has arrived! How very exquisite! Such food I

have never before been exposed to!" And so, the two

families became one, with little Phyllis in the memories of

both.

~ Chapter Eleven ~

The months had passed almost all at once, the change in the family not forgotten, but thought upon with a more confident and accepting mind with the knowledge that Phyllis had entered into the next journey in life. Whenever the family entered the room formerly owned by the dear girl, her presence was warmly felt by each member, and although she herself was gone, her spirit remained, reminding each that sorrow was not the answer. Felicity had frequently visited since the funeral to pay respects to her sister, and sometimes she found herself inspired to write at the same desk used by Phyllis, and would resume conversation with the remainder of the household some hours after leaving what became her sanctuary, only to return to her new home where she was greeted by William. His busy schedule had at first caused issues of solitary moments lasting far too long, yet as the marriage progressed, and the two became closer both in spirit and person, his days were spent more freely at their residence when possible. The most exciting development in their union, however, was their new aspiration to expand the family; the two had been trying for a child only a little while before Felicity was with child and she had told as much to her elder sister first:

"Oh, Adelaide! It is such a wonderful yet terrifying experience, but I am sure that with you to look towards and for support, I shall not struggle too much. I only wish Phyllis could be here so that I may introduce her to her new niece or nephew." She held her hands reverently over her stomach, looking solemnly towards the window - this was often where she looked when thinking of her sister for the air was alive and welcoming.

"She will be here with us as she always is," was Adelaide's sisterly response accepted with much appreciation.

Only months later was Felicity blessed with a daughter - Elizabeth Mae – who resembled her Aunt Phyllis in that she was quiet and good. Multiple members of the family had visited in her first few days of life, even some distant relatives close with Lady Augusta, who, although excited for the successful birth, expressed her disappointment for the lack of a male heir. Felicity had already begun to feel this guilt the moment her daughter entered this world, but her husband had assured her they would soon try again, and that for now he was perfectly content with Elizabeth Mae. Lady Augusta had been assured also that a male heir would be produced by both husband and wife, and so she was left to enjoy the selection of people around the room whom she would tell them forwardly their faults.

The same and more collection of people had gathered at the church the first Sunday after the birth for the christening of Elizabeth Mae who had been clothed in a white dress with silk fastenings. Petite fingers curled around Felicity's own as she walked her down the aisle with her husband. The ceremony, although not lasting long and certainly not extravagant to any extent, had proven to be on a beautiful day, the sun shining outside suggested to the family that Phyllis was also present in spirit.

Also at the christening was Nathaniel who had married Kitty, Felicity's younger sister, only a few weeks previously. The union had not been expected by any or all, and Lady August had clearly expressed her utter disgust at Kitty's choice of suitor, for she had been aware of the problems he had caused with Felicity. Dear reader, I am certain you are curious as to how this union came to be considering the opposition towards it. The simple answer is that the two had eloped, and had Kitty partook in such an event previously, Mrs Thorpe would have cast her off, but she could not bear to lose another daughter. And so, the union had been accepted by Mr and Mrs Thorpe, and Felicity, although now in love with her husband, still found it difficult to see the two together, for she was aware of Nathaniel's true self, but she felt certain that she would never tell Kitty, for the sin of divorce seemed much worse in her mind. More importantly than that, Kitty seemed happy after such a terrible circumstance, and Felicity would never forgive herself for ruining such contentment.

Over the following years, much was to be said about Felicity and William, although Lady Augusta, still alive much to the dislike of the family, expressed on multiple occasions her dissatisfaction with the couple having three more little girls! How had it been possible that no male heir had been born, when Kitty had produced the most beautiful and dear baby boy within just their first year of marriage, and both a boy and a girl had followed on from such an achievement. With such a success, their elopement had almost nearly been forgotten, save for one or two snide remarks from the Great Aunt, who wished that the union had been carried out in the traditional way. A least Felicity had done so. Adelaide had also birthed another boy, Henry, but the two had decided two to be adequate enough when Adelaide became ill one summer, and never quite recovered.

Dear reader, I must tell you about the manuscript William had sent to be published, which it had been, and although it never sold more than two hundred copies, the book itself was followed by a set of short stories aimed at young women which sold double, and provided Felicity with such pride in addition to a small income, which although not necessary due to the immensity of William's own, made Felicity feel as though she really was capable of almost everything a man could do.

And so ends this story of Felicity Giles, formerly Miss Felicity Thorpe of Thorpe Hall, but her achievements continued to prosper along with her writing and children continued to the end of her days.

Enjoyed Felicity? The sequel is out now!

Turn over for a sneak peak!

~ Chapter One ~

Adelaide Thorpe, if you are not familiar with our protagonist, belongs to three younger sisters: Felicity, Kitty, and dear little Phyllis. Their strong relationship had been developed in the many years in which they had played and worked side by side before Adelaide had left her beautiful country home in order to create her own family with a successful businessman, Nicholas Ramsey, who lived in the neighbouring town. Their union had begun three summers before when she was entering her 18th year in life, and he his 25th, and had initially been received with reluctance and even fury from her Great Aunt Augusta.

Lady Augusta, as she was known to the majority of Bath, had acquired a large fortune following the death of her husband a few years prior, and was considered an opinionated, and consequently troublesome, figure between the members of the Thorpe family, excepting of course Adelaide's mother, Margaret, who was so enthralled by the wealth and status of the old woman that she found in her heart more acceptance for her forward, and often rude, ways of conversing. Some level of ability in tolerating a conversation with her Aunt had Adelaide succeeded in attaining, and she often found herself mediating between her and her sister Felicity, as the two found themselves more often than not conflicted on one matter or another. Through this, Adelaide had fulfilled her duty as the elder sister to protect and guide the younger girls, even though at times this proved difficult.

Returning to the hesitation shown by Lady Augusta, she had verbally demonstrated her opposition to his status and youthful age on multiple occasions, yet the couple seemed almost unaffected by her resistance. In each other, they had found a trusting and content marriage, and for the romantic nature of their hearts, this suited them quite perfectly. And so, with a frowning personality sat rigid in the front row of the church, Adelaide Thorpe became Adelaide Ramsey and promised to stand by Nicholas for as long as they both shall live. With the exception of Lady Augusta, the church was alive with merriment and celebration, as the two walked arm in arm down the aisle towards the colossal doors and into the carriage, and the day had been spent with little thought of the miser, much to her own dismay.

Within a year of that joyous day, Adelaide and Nicholas were blessed with their firstborn. Looking down at the babe in her arms, she was met with small, delicate features and a prevailing sense of innocence in Katarina's eyes. Her soft features imitated that of her mother's, as well as her quiet temperament, yet Nicholas was the preferred parent as he spoiled her due to an abundance of love he had not the pleasure of giving to anyone but his wife and daughter.

For two years the three lived quite happily in their sizeable home, along with their two servants, in a town quite close to Adelaide's family; this pleased the Thorpe household as it meant that the sisters would not be separated to a great extent.

Our story begins on a day quite close to Katarina's second birthday, with the Ramsey's and Lady Augusta sat politely within the confinement of the parlour. The Great Aunt was sipping her tea at an immense speed; Adelaide had learned of the woman's mannerisms and their meanings long ago, and so she knew that her haste demonstrated that her Aunt had something of importance to tell them, and was simply trying to be courteous when offered the beverage before she began. And began she did:

"Now, Adelaide, you know how much I adore little Katarina, but don't you feel as though there is something quite the miss?" Adelaide positioned her mouth as though to speak, but was cut off before she could utter a syllable. "Not only would it be beneficial in Katarina's upbringing, but to have a boy would secure your family line and provide opportunity for the both of you! As you know, I, myself, birthed six strong boys, one of whom being your father, who, though sweet at heart, has no practical mind about him. Perhaps you better have two boys minimum."

"Aunt Augusta," Adelaide began, in the tenderest voice she could manage, for that was the best way to communicate an opposing opinion to her visitor. "At the moment, we do not feel it necessary to bring another child into the house."

"Why ever not? There are only benefits for such an action; I am proof enough of that! You are at such a prime age for childbirth; you shan't be twenty and one forever." She placed the teacup down harshly, twittering away to herself in shock. "First, you marry without my blessing to a man below what you could have achieved," she began, husband and wife suddenly finding themselves blushing. "And then you refuse to provide for your family! It's disgraceful, and I'm sure that your mother would agree with me; that woman has such sense in these matters. Although, of course, I am still discombobulated as to how she could allow such a union as yours to happen! I would never have allowed my own daughter, if I had had one, to partake in such a demotion of status as has occurred here."

"I understand your thoughts on our marriage, Aunt Augusta, but the fact of the matter is, we are already married, quite happily so, and therefore, I do not understand what you expect," Adelaide managed, feeling as though the difficulty in remaining polite to her Aunt's standards had become almost impossible.

"I expect little, for you have promised yourselves to each other but what I do propose is a way to fix, in a way, what you have started. You shall need a son in order to carry on Nicholas' business, for Katarina cannot do so, and she will be of no use for another fifteen years when we can begin to find potential suitors for her."

"She will only be seventeen at that point?" Nicholas questioned. Of course, he knew that it was expected for girls to marry young, but Adelaide had been eighteen which he personally deemed a more appropriate age for marriage.

"Rather late if you ask me," the old lady began. "Perhaps I should begin my search a year earlier." Adelaide could not help but wonder if Lady Augusta would still be alive after another fourteen years, but the family had accepted that she was quite talented at defying death, and so the young girl assumed that questioning the likelihood would in fact be futile. "I expected some reluctance from the both of you, I must admit, and so I propose this: should you fail in providing a male heir, I shall remove you from my will, which, I can promise you, involves a considerable sum." Nicholas and Adelaide had never been materialistic in the slightest, and preferred to live a simple, though comfortable, life, and so this did not have the grand impact in which the old lady hoped to achieve.

"We shall think on it," Adelaide promised.

"I suppose that is all I can ask of you; the two of you never seem to be traditional in any sense. That being said, this was much easier than it was for your mother to find a husband for Felicity; now that girl really is trouble! I do feel sorry for the man," and she continued her twittering, Adelaide and Nicholas both trying to follow along, though equally unsure as to whether they were supposed to be listening; Lady Augusta seemed quite in her own world.

Until she left to return to her stately home, she spent the remainder of her time complaining of people and situations, making Adelaide and her husband quite uncomfortable yet unable to do anything about the matter. After a further three quarters of an hour, she found that she had exhausted as much as possible for the time being and requested her carriage be prepared so that she may return home to the relief of the young couple.

The company of the old woman was replaced with that of their two year old daughter, Katarina, who paralleled Lady Augusta significantly in both energy and optimism, as she bounded into the room which contained her parents as soon as she heard the closing of the door. Her coping mechanism for tolerating the Great Aunt was to avoid her as much as possible, for little Katarina was sometimes frightened by her loud and authoritative voice.

"Come here, little one," Adelaide said, reaching out her loving arms to hold her child close to her, grateful for the innocent smile on her toddler's face which appeared even more refreshing after having been with their tiresome guest for so long.

"Food," Katarina said.

"She has her priorities all clear," Nicholas laughed, tickling her before taking her from her mother to hold her himself.

"Daddy!" she chimed.

"Shall we go and ask the servants to lay out dinner?" he asked Adelaide, putting his other arm around his wife. The three of them appeared picturesque together, each smiling face presenting a member of the ideal loving family unit.

Only a little while later, a meal had been prepared and the family was sat around their quaint little table. Grace was said before Katarina excitedly ate as much as she was allowed, and Adelaide and Nicholas made sure every morsel had been eaten, for they both knew what it was like to survive on little and so they had found an appreciation for all that they had.

The meal passed not in silence, but in conversation, as the family believed in communication and developing relationships, rather than a strict code of conduct as one would expect at the dinner table. It was used as an opportunity to speak of the happenings of their day, for Adelaide remained at home with Katarina, and Nicholas worked in the office all day and sometimes into the evenings. It also, for this particular reason, was a large portion of the time that Nicholas had with his daughter to whom he was very much attached, and at times he even regretted being so passive in her upbringing due to his occupation, yet he knew that his wife was a wonderful mother and their daughter would want for nothing.

"I shall have to leave earlier in the morning, I'm afraid," Nicholas said, being reminded from his train of thought to inform her. "We have some new clients which could prove revolutionary to the company, and so there is a rather large amount of preparation to complete."

"Compete," Katarina repeated, a smugness clouding her face.

"Well done, darling," Adelaide said, encouraging any lexical attempt from the toddler, no matter how flawed. Then, turning towards Nicholas: "Would you wake me before you leave so that I may see you?"

"Of course I shall, for I could not leave to start my day without first spending a moment with my beautiful wife," he reached out for her hand to kiss it softly, their eyes alight with their love for each other.

"Eww!" Katarina squealed, creating a reaction of laughter from her parents. "Kiss!" she said.

"Now, I think that Katarina is perhaps ready for sleepy time," Adelaide said, removing her fingers from Nicholas' clasp to pick the child up. "I shall take her to bed myself tonight." Nicholas nodded in response, watching in awe as his family left the room. He couldn't help but think back to what Lady Augusta had mentioned; he thought not of the will and the threat, but of expanding their family. He already had so much love for his little Katarina, and so he imagined having more children to give that same love to. Adelaide had grown up with three sisters, and having been witness to their close connection to one another, he wanted nothing more than for his own dear little Katarina to experience a similar childhood. Having little family of his own, he also wished to create a full and exciting setting in their home to accommodate his family-orientated nature which had been for so long neglected, though not due to his own fault.

I hope you enjoyed the opening to the sequel! To read on, Adelaide is available on Amazon in paperback and eBook form!

Printed in Great Britain
by Amazon

41179005R00098